The Amaze 'N Apple Adventure

AMAZE 'N APPLES

Created by
Royal Oak Farm

Co-Written & Illustrated by
Kym Ann Mack

Print information available on the last page

Rev. date: 03/21/2016

To order additional copies of this book, contact:
Xlibris
1-888-795-4274
www.Xlibris.com
Orders@Xlibris.com

The Royal Oak Family dedicates this book to

the LORD JESUS CHRIST,

FOR HIS GLORY,

AND

To His Servant, Peter Bianchini, Sr., who thru the Lord's resources, wisdom and strength, led him to provide a place of beauty, joy and memories, for all of God's children to enjoy.

The Amaze 'N Apple Adventure

Created By

Royal Oak Farm

Co-Written & Illustrated By

Kym Ann Mack

In a small village, there lived a kind farmer and his young daughter, SnowSweet.

He planted an apple orchard where families came from near and far to pick his wonderful apples.

One day, while the farmer was tending his orchard, he had a thought. "I know," he said to SnowSweet, "I'll make a maze out of apple trees! No one has been in an apple tree maze before!"

The farmer planted the apple tree maze with the help of SnowSweet and her farm friends, Braeburn bunny, Crispin and MacIntosh the alpacas, Gala and her guinea hen gals, and Zestar the Goat.

Every year the little trees grew taller and bigger. From the sky, the trees formed the shape of a giant apple. The farmer called his creation "AMAZE 'N APPLES."

In the center of the maze, the farmer built a tower. "We need a place for people to go if they get lost or scared," he told SnowSweet. "From the tower, they can see which path to take."

"I have an idea," said SnowSweet. "Let's put our *Book of Wisdom* in the tower. We always read it when we need help!"

"Good idea, SnowSweet," the farmer said, and the *Book of Wisdom* was placed in the tower.

Finally, the big day came. The trees were fully-grown, and the apples were ripe. The maze was ready to open.

"It's an AMAZE 'N Day!" SnowSweet announced to her farm friends.

"Let's go everyone; there are apples to be picked!"

Zestar the goat jumped right over Braeburn bunny in his eagerness to help. "Zestar," laughed SnowSweet,

"You pick the apples on this side. Braeburn, umm... you can pick over there!"

Crispin and MacIntosh, the alpaca brothers, came running with their apple baskets, happy to help.

"When your baskets are full," instructed SnowSweet, "take them to the barn. But the paths in the maze are tricky, so don't get lost!"

Zestar and Braeburn were busy picking. "Mmmm," Zestar said, "These apples look yummy. Maybe I'll try just one." Chomp, Chomp, Chomp! "These apples are AMAZE 'N!" he thought. He quickly ate one, then another, then another. Zestar couldn't stop.

Just then, Gala and her guinea hen gals came running down the path toward Zestar. "Oh my, my, my!" exclaimed Gala. "You are n-n-not supposed to be eating all those apples! We must g-g-go and tell SnowSweet!" Clucking loudly, they scurried off to find SnowSweet, leaving Zestar behind.

Zestar, feeling bad, curled up under his pile of apple cores. "Aww, Zestar, what's wrong?" asked Braeburn, poking his head out from between the trees.

"I know I disobeyed because I ate the apples," Zestar confessed. "I was supposed to pick them not eat them, and I'm afraid SnowSweet will find out."

"Aww Zestar, don't be afraid," said Braeburn, "I
think you would feel better if you told SnowSweet
what you did."

Suddenly, there was a rumble in the distance. "Wait! Did you hear that?" Braeburn asked. "It sounds like THUNDER! Oh dear, I don't like thunder!"

Another clap of thunder sounded; Zestar and Braeburn both started shaking. "Let's go find SnowSweet!" they cried as they ran through the maze.

"Hurry!" SnowSweet called, when she saw Zestar and Braeburn coming toward her on the path. "There's a storm coming, and I'm scared. Let's get to the tower where we'll be safe. The *Book of Wisdom* is there, and it will help us."

The wind started blowing harder, and the sky turned dark as they ran down the path.

Gala and her guinea hen gals were still searching for SnowSweet when a strong wind blew the shirt off a nearby scarecrow, and it plopped right down on top of Gala! "Where did everyone go?" Gala screeched as she ran around in circles. She was quite a sight! The guinea hen gals squawked, running in all directions from the strange creature chasing them.

Nearing the tower, SnowSweet and her friends saw the strange looking creature run into the clearing making a terrible squawking noise. Crispin and MacIntosh were prancing excitedly, trying not to step on it.

"What is that?" cried Zestar. SnowSweet rushed to look. She put her foot on a trailing sleeve and out popped Gala!

"Oh, my, my, my!" cried Gala. "I was trying to find you, SnowSweet, to tell you that Zestar was eating all the apples, and suddenly, I couldn't see a thing!"

SnowSweet couldn't help laughing as she tried to calm her friends.

"Ka-boom!" another clap of thunder sounded, and the rain started pouring. "Quick, everyone, get to the tower!" she yelled.

"Storms make me feel afraid," said SnowSweet, as she snuggled with her friends in the tower.

"Us, too," they replied, but Zestar and Gala realized there was something else they were afraid of too.

"I was afraid to tell you that I ate the apples when I was supposed to be picking them. Will you forgive me?" asked Zestar.

"And I'm afraid that I'm a t-t-tattletale! Will you forgive me, too?" asked Gala.

"Of course I will!" SnowSweet responded, giving her friends a big hug.

"Just then, the farmer, wet from the rain, came running up the tower stairs. When he reached the top, a bolt of lightening lit up the sky, and SnowSweet and her friends started shaking.

26

Seeing their fear, the kind farmer knew what to do. He pulled out the *Book of Wisdom* they had placed in the tower and began to read.

After listening to his words, SnowSweet and her friends didn't feel so afraid anymore. The rain stopped and an AMAZE 'N rainbow appeared over the orchard.

"I'll remember to read the *Book of Wisdom* the next time I'm afraid," SnowSweet said, and all her friends agreed!

Dear Reader,

We sincerely hope that you have enjoyed, "The Amaze 'N Apple Adventure." This story was written to teach children about the importance of forgiveness and how to deal with fear, but it also showcases where imagination can lead, to the development of the country's first apple tree maze. If your family would like to participate in the real adventure of Amaze 'N Apples, we invite you to visit us at Royal Oak Farm. We look forward to seeing you!

For His Glory,

The Royal Oak Farm Family

ROYAL OAK FARM'S
AMAZE 'N APPLES

RoyalOakFarmOrchard.com

Amaze 'N Apples

is located at

Royal Oak Farm Apple Orchard

In

Harvard, IL

The maze is open to the public during the Fall. For more information please

visit

<u>RoyalOakFarmOrchard.com</u>

Printed in the United States
By Bookmasters